ARESCANIUS

ET INGRESSUM DEAMONIUM

SANKALP VAISHNAV

ISBN 979-888606458-2

Contents

Preface

Sanskar -

Thank you for keeping this book with you at this time and for giving your valuable time to this book . I am very lucky that you have bought this book . Ignore some minor mistakes in this book . Because this is our puzzle book . And we wrote it with all our heart . This book is not complete yet , the next part of this book will come soon . So once more thank you wholeheartedly.

Acknowledgements

After one chapter you will get an idea about how story moving on and how bigger it will get . In this whole journey of my book writing , I would like to thank my brother **SANSKAR VAISHNAV** who is also **Co-AUTHOR** of this book , without his guidance and conviction this book will never get a proper and developed direction of story . I am very glad he molded this story into a better piece of work . I would like to thank my father and mother , they appreciate my work and effort on book . without their support and inspiration my book never got published . Thank to my family for giving me this vital opportunity .

Prologue

A kingdom known as SKYRIM . SKYRIM was ruled by a king named RALPH MURPHY . Ralph was a very cruel and ruthless king . Ralph used to oppress his countrymen a lot . In every six months Ralph recruit amry to attack on neighboring kingdom . On attacking small kingdom and villages his army became sufficient to attack on large scale and get a huge victory . The childrens after the age 14 were forcefully told to join the army for battles . Ralph increases the tax due expenses of war every six months , kingdom treasuries were about to empty . People were suffering from starvation . Ralph keeps invading to his neighboring kingdom even after knowning that his people were dying from starvation and loss of manpower on war . After Two years of this series of war Skyrim population reduced to half , this peroid is called BLACK YEAR of Skyrim .

CHAPTER ONE

ANCILLARY

A MAN WILL FIGHT HARDER FOR HIS INTEREST THAN FOR HIS RIGHTS .- NAPOLEAN BONAPARTE

One day Ralph decided to increase tax and started giving more priorities to royalmen and chruch . The day came when skyrimian to raise there voice because the price was increased by triple folds , they have already suffered enough on their past days now it was the time to stand against Ralph . Ralph didn't knew that indoors of his own kingdom , seed of hate began to thrive in heart of every people .

A group of people formed a revolutionary association called GOLDEN WING . The leader of GOLDEN WING was NATHAN SMITH . NATHAN was very skilled and trained soldier of ralph's army , he later on promoted as lieutenant general of ralph's army . Now he had all the controls and informations of skyrimian army. Ralph promote him as lieutenant general because Nathan's skill to analyse war was so good and accurate . Ralph was very impressed by him and trusted him very much and had never thought that one day he will be a revolutionary leader . The question is why nathan will be going betray him . Nathan had everything that a man may ever want . Nathan had a good life that he always wanted . He had two children LUIS and OLIVIA and a beautiful wife DIANE .

1.1 HISTORY OF NATHAN

Nathan was born in ROLAND . It was a state comes under SKYRIM . Nathan's parents were very poor , his father was a farmer and mother was a housewife . In the beginning of adulthood of nathan he used to work on a blacksmith market . He was a hardworking and dedicated worker . Shopowner was very impressed by his hard work . Shopowner treat him as his own son because he never had one . His wife died on the battle of skyrim . so, he never had a children .

1.1.1 TURNING POINT OF NATHANS LIFE

One day ,

After six months of previous battle now it's time for recruitment for army . Nathan never wanted to be part of skyrimian amry , he was happy with job and his life . He never wanted to lose it . But unfortunately the time came . He forcefully joined the army and prepared for next battle . He always remembered his past life . He always remembered his owner's love and anger for him . Nathan always imagined his owner as his father . Nathan's skills and intelligence was so good that on his very first battle he defeated enemy troops without loss of many soldiers , due to which Ralph gave him a special position on his assembly . Ralph never wanted him to leave his army . Actually , there is a rule that every natives of skyrim must work for army at least five year . After five year of Nathan as a soldier now it's time for him to leave the army . But , Ralph never wanted him to leave so he gave him a high position in his army . But , nathan wants his past life back and refuses his request .

Conversation between Ralph and Nathan inside court :-

RALPH(With order) :- You are a great

warrior that every kingdom want to have , your dedication towards SKYRIM is very impressive and in future skyrim need a warrior like you. Now the time came for you to leave the army but , I ask you to serve skyrim forever and I am right now promoting you as a head of our one of best "GOLDEN WING". GOLDEN WING is a organisation over a thousands of brave soldier .

NATHAN(With respect) :-

My lord I had showed you my effort , hardwork , dedication and devotion towards SKYRIM but now it's time to end this .All I want is my past life back . I Served skyrim for five year and I am very much glad and proud for that . But I request you to please permit me to live that life again .

RALPH(With anger) :-

Did you said request

Nathan :-

Yes , my king

Ralph(with anger) :-

Do you even imagine what are the consequences of your words . How dare you to refuse my command , you pathetic animal . Do you even imagine what honour and position you just refused . GOLDEN WING is one the best organisation that SKYRIM ever get .

Ralph(with anger) to one of his soldier :-

Arrest him and put him into the prison

Nathan was arrested . After knowning that nathan had a opportunity to beacome Golden wing leader . Some people in assembly got jealous and had thought that king is giving nathan more priority to him than other of his subordinate . Everyone was against the king's decision and nathan's too . meanwhile , one of his assembly member named REMY was getting less attention from king due to nathan's work in assembly . Remy was a head commander of Ralph's army and he couldn't accept the fact that someone is more important to the king istead of him . After knowning that Nathan was arrested , he decided to negotiate with nathan and offered a situation with both of their benefits .

Conversation between Nathan and Remy inside jail :-

Remy to Nathan :-

I have an offer for you .

Nathan(Ignoring):-

Hmmm .

Remy :-

Belive me it is beneficial to both of us .

Nathan :-

What do you want ?

Remy :-

I will give you freedom and your family . But , for one cost you will have to lead Golden wing and you will make golden wing a revolutionary association instead of ralph's army .

Nathan :-
When we are going to do this .
Remy :-
Just follow my command .
But for now just be patient.

Next day,

Remy requested to Ralph , that Nathan is a great warrior and we need his skills in our coming battles .

Ralph :-
It will never going to happen .
Remy :-

Just think without his strategy and tactics how you suppose to win . I said to nathan that you will serve SKYRIM forever . And if you resist and refuse your family won't see next morning .

Ralph :-
He agreed or not
Remy :-
Yes my lord , he agreed .

Next day ,

Remy to Nathan :-
You are free now .
Nathan :-
Just tell me when will we proceed to our plan .
Remy :-
You will get to know when time comes .

After six months ,

Nathan was a leader of GOLDEN WING . He setup a meeting for important members of golden wing. It consist of five members . Except Remy and nathan no one knowns about the rest of three members . Nathan proposed an idea that they will setup a negotiation with opponent kingdom and making sure that no one knowns about it . Negotiation was successfully done and the opponent kingdom was agreed .

1.2 BATTLE OF BETRAYAL

Battle day ,

Nathan lead golden wing where Remy leads Ralph's army . Remy sent troops in a wave form . On first hand , he sent armies who didn't knew about the plan as result the loyal soldiers were died and only traitor in armies were left . Nathan send a black somke which signifies the signal of deception . Ralph recognized the smoke and already knew that he is bieng betrayed by his own soldiers BUT , HOW RALPH ALREADY KNEW ABOUT THIS DECEPTION AND NOT TOOK ANY ACTION YET .

1 week ago ,

Actually , Remy CHEATED golden wing and opponent kingdom . The meeting or negotiation day , at the counsil there were five members in which Remy was also invited . Next day, Remy leaks every details of their plan to the enemy of Ralph . Someone gave this message to Ralph , that was how Ralph already knew everything . Ralph gave a proposal to golden wing and some traitors that he will give anything that they want But they have to give their loyality towards him . Those who not agreed were killed instantly .

On the day of battle ,

Everyone in golden wing betrayed Nathan and captured him . Enemy was also defeated . Day after battle , Ralph announced Nathan's punishment to take his head apart . Nathan died in front of every citzen even his family , his owner and his children and wife . The moment was full of sadness and dark . Everyone in his relation were crying . It was such painfull and terrifying moment for everyone . Nathan was a good person and a good father . All he ever wanted to go back to his home and live a happy life with his family . Ralph gave an example to people that if anyone will ever try to betray him , they will get killed . Meanwhile, Remy announce the name of that three unknown men that was WILLIAM HARTLAND , ROBERT CATER AND SEBASTIAN HANSEN .

CHAPTER TWO

EQUIVALENT EXCHANGE

Nathan's death is an example for people who were trying to stand against Ralph . But somewhere in skyrim people still want freedom .

Somewhere in SKYRIM ,

WILLIAM HARTLAND , ROBERT CARTER AND SEBASTIAN HANSEN were hiding in country . Ralph set a two million rio bounty for those who found them .

NOTE :-

RIO IS A CURRENCY OF SKYRIM .

Meanwhile ,

William , Robert and Sebastian re-established golden wing . They started their association from Roland . Roland was a good start for this association because of Nathan's death . Everyone in Roland respected Nathan and saw him as a idol . Everyone support Nathan and love him . They felt that Nathan was innocent . After re-establishment of golden wing everyone in Roland support them and join golden wing . Women and children were excluded . After the support of Roland towards golden wing became huge and news of golden wing spread all over skyrim . Initially golden wing used to rob royal treasury and donate it to the poor people . After this small small efforts golden wing became huge concern for Ralph . Ralph got annoyed by golden wing and want a permanent solution . Golden wing keep robbing and interfere royal matter . Finally , Ralph decided to declare battle against Golden wing . Golden wing thought that there goal was succeeded . They finally got opportunity to hold attention on Skyrim citizen . Ralph gave five months for preparation of attack . There was a reason behind five months . Actually , After two month ralph going to attack neighbour kingdom and recruit army , then next month he will be going to make a deal with an ally . But , Golden wing had a plan too that they will also going to make a deal with an ally .

After Two months ,

A very beautiful and marvelous kingdom called WISTER was ally of skyrim . If the deal is successfully accomplished then it will be a big achievement for Ralph's army . But, Wister was also an ally of golden wing . Sebastian is a friend of Wister's king Leonard Martin . Coincidentally , both ralph and golden wing having a same ally . Leonard was very clever and intelligent king , he proposed an idea .

•

LEONARD to RALPH and GOLDEN WING :-

I have an offer for you both that I will organise an man to man fight on my arena . You both will get only one chance . GOLDEN WING will have to choose one fighter from there group .

Golden wing chose Sebastian as there fighter where Ralph chose himself as a fighter . They both are very highly skilled fighter . They both had a great fight . It was very difficult to predict the winner on fight . After many rounds both ralph and sebastian got tired . Finally Sebastian knock him but Ralph doesn't gave up and spit blood on Sebastian face . Sebastian got distracted and defeated . Ralph doesn't kill sebastian and said .

RALPH(with anger) TO SEBASTIAN :-

I'm forgiving you this time . But it is not the end of our fight . I will kill you on battleground . Until then I will let you live .

SEBASTIAN(with anger) to RALPH :-

Time will tell you who is going to die . you defeat me because of your cheap move . If you have any courage then defeat me without cheating me .

RALPH(with anger) to SEBASTIAN :-

Mark my words .

LEONARD to everyone :-

As we all know that Ralph is our winner . so as I said ,I will give twenty percent of my army to Ralph on his battle against Golden Wing .

RALPH(with respect):-

My pleasure old friend .

Next day ,

Ralph took soldiers which Leonard gave him and departured for skyrim . But Golden wing stayed in castle of Wister making a plan for battle . Now , this will be very difficult for them to win against Ralph . Wisters army was the last hope . But Leonard proposed an idea and that was last hope for Golden wing .

LEONARD to GOLDEN WING :-

I have an idea .

SEBASTIAN to LEONARD :-

Tell us .

LEONARD to GOLDEN WING :-

A god called NOHA , he is very popular god in western side . You have to visit a city called MANCAY . where you have to serve your devotion to god noha . He will fullfill any wish you want .

After one month they arrived to **MANCAY** *.*

Where William , Robert and Sebastian perform rituals and served Noha for six month due to which war had been cancelled . After six months , After long devotion and dedication finally god Noha appeared .

GOD NOHA :-

I can give you anything you want , but for only one cost , that you have to give me something which will be equally valuable to your wish . To maintain the law of equivalence you have to sacrifice something valuable as your wish . You have to think within one day .

After two hour ,

William and Robert made a plan for "equivalent exchange" wish . William and Robert both invited Sebastian and whole army for dinner . After dinner , SAKE (alcoholic beverage) was served to Sebastian and his army . But , Sebastian refused to take it . Few minutes later , everyone were intoxicated and lost their consciousness and fell in ground except Sebastian . Sebastian found that there was something suspicious regarding Wlliam and Robert hence he resisted to take sake . When Sebastian's army was unconscious , William and Robert burned them alive . Somehow Sebastian escaped .

Sebastian will never forgot their fraud .

Next day ,

William and Robert wished to bring all soldiers alive ,

God NOHA fullfilled Sebastian's wish by giving him died army of immortal soldiers . Now Golden Wing is having an immortal army .

CHAPTER THREE

REVENGE IS COLD

REVENGE IS A DISH BEST SERVED COLD .

- CHARLES PERIGORD

<u>PART ONE</u>

PRESENT DAY ,

After Sebastian got betrayed by William and Robert , he was hiding in Wister castle . Meanwhile , Robert and William were preparing for the third battle of skyrim . Golden Wing sent an messenger to Ralph giving him a chance to surrender . Ralph disagreed and wanted battle . Golden wing give him two month for preparations .

After Nathan death ,

4.1 Nathan's family after his death .

Nathan had two children Luis and olivia . After Nathan's death his wife was died due to Heart attack . Nathan's younger daughter olivia had an intellectual disability after her father's death . Nathan's children were living with their grandfather until their grandfather died . After their grandfather death Sebastian adopted them . Luis is a good brother who always take care of his younger sister Olivia . Olivia doesn't even bath and eat properly . Luis was always there to support and help her . It is very hard for Luis because Olivia doesn't even talk properly . At the age of seven Luis had given big responsibilities on his shoulders . His childhood was not like other child . No one can ever get how painful it was for him to live with such a pain . After his grandfather's death he was working on pawn shop and raised money . Luis and Olivia living a poor life . Sometimes they don't have enough money to buy foods . Luis was matured from his very young age .

4.2 Sebastian as father .

After re-establishing of Golden wing in Roland , Sebastian saw a kid working on a pawn shop and said .

•

SEBASTIAN TO LUIS :-

Who are you kid and why are you working on a pawn shop ?

LUIS TO SEBASTIAN :-

My name is luis smith .

SEBASTIAN TO LUIS :-

Smith hah .

So you are probably son of Nathan smith . Your father was a great warrior and you don't deserve this life because everything your father had done was only for you . He always wanted to meet you but it won't happend . I know what's going inside you . I have also gone through lots of thing and like you I also lost my father at very young age .

LUIS (crying) TO SEBATIAN :-

No you don't know anything .

Luis was crying and ran away from there . Sebastian felt guilty for Nathan's death . He thought that due to him Nathan died . After making Golden wing a huge army . Sebastian decided to adopt Luis and olivia . Luis and Olivia are now the adopted children of sebastian .

PRESENT DAY ,

Sebastian is hiding in Wister castle and Leonard provided him protection . Before battle , Leonard decided to negotiate with both Golden wing and Ralph . Negotiation date will be done after one week .

One week later *,*

All the kings of continents came and join world biggest royal assembly on Wister castle . Everyone in assembly know that Golden wing having a huge immortal army . So they suggested Ralph that it's better to surrender and to save lives of many soldiers . But , Ralph refuses the suggestions of members and prepared for battle .

RALPH TO EVERY MEMBERS :-

I not afraid from death neither his army . I will fight till the end of the battle . I know how painful it is to be an unworthy and weak king . In the past I am the weakest king of the Skyrim's history . I always remember my past when people call me an "unworthy king of skyrim" . But now things has been changed people call me the most brutal and ruthless king ever of Skyrim . They forget that my cruelity , brutality and ruthlessness was born from their hatred and I never will forget that . The people of skyrim who turned me from innocent to brutal . From then , only thing I have is my army and they are ready for battle . Battle is the only thing that I want .

Everyone in assembly appreciate Ralph's speech and agreed for battle . The Assembly was consist of William , Robert and Sebastian too . William and Robert cannot do anything because Sebastian was under the protection of Leonard's bodygaurds .

After assembly Ralph met with Luis and asked him .

RALPH TO LUIS :-

Who are you and what are you doing here ?

LUIS TO RALPH :-

My name is Luis Smith and Sebastian has adopted me and now he is my father .

RALPH TO LUIS :-

So , your surname is smith that means you are the son of Nathan Smith .

RALPH (crying):-

If my daughter was still alive she might be at your age . My daughter was the only happiness that I ever got . But she died by some assassins . "Why god why won't you take me instead of daughter" . From that moment my life was meaningless which turned me into what I am now "a cruel king" .

Sebastian came and took Luis away from there .

SEBASTIAN TO RALPH :-

I heard your story . It was very painful and heart broking story . But it was fate ,was not your fault .

RALPH TO SEBASTIAN :-

But why me . Why only with me ?

RALPH TO SEBASTIAN :-

I got some strange and dark vibe from Leonard . Stay alert !

After half hour later Ralph proceeded for skyrim .

After five hour ,

All the members had dinner . Meanwhile , Robert and William plotted a plan to kill Luis rather than Sebastian because Sebastian was under the protection Wister's soldiers and his adopted son Luis wasn't . Few minutes after dinner Robert and some of his soldier gone to take Luis down . Luis was surronded by Robert's soldiers there was no way to escape than suddenly Robert took step forward and stapped Luis on his abdominal part . Luis instantly died . William and Robert with there army were escaped after this incident from Wister castle .

PART TWO

After few minutes sebastian found his son on floor covered with blood and his heat beat and his pulse stopped . He never knew that things will go that worst . Sebastian thought that it was his mistake to adopt Luis as his son which results his death . Sebastian didn't get happiness all his life . His whole life was suffering and was painful . He got betrayed from his friends , his inital mission was failed and now his adopted son is died . Sebastian was broken inside . After few hours Sebastian washed Luis body and for the last time Olivia met his brother . Olivia's brain was not developed so she couldn't understand what is death . Olivia embrace Luis and tried to wake him up . After this emotional moment Sebastian took her away from there . Leonard was also emotionally connected to Luis . Leonard said to Sebastian that he will bring Luis back .

•

LEONARD TO SEBASTIAN :-

Is your son very precious to you . I can bring him back .

SEBASTIAN TO LEONARD :-

HOW ???

LEONARD TO SEBASTIAN :-

Remember six month ealier , I told you about God Noha . But , there is a another being who is enough powerful to bring back your son . But he is a demon called Alucard "the Demon king" .

SEBASTIAN TO LEONARD :-

I will do anything to bring him back alive .

After some rituality Leonard summons Alucard and told him about Luis .

Alucard said that ...

ALUCARD :-

I can bring Luis back to life but only on one cost .

SEBASTIAN TO ALUCARD :-

I can do anything . Whatever it takes .

ALUCARD TO SEBASTIAN :-

I just want one day of your life .

But , there is one side effect that your son will grow old quicker than you .

SEBASTIAN TO ALUCARD :-

Sure .

But I also want one thing from you .

ALUCARD TO SEBASTIAN :-

What's your another wish .

SEBASTIAN TO ALUCARD :-

Tell me a way to defeat immortal army .

ALUCARD TO SEBASTIAN :-

There is a way to defeat immortal army .

Dead army was born from angelic power and to encounter that you need my demonic power . Demonic power is the only way to defeat immortal army . I will give you and rest of your army my powers the in exchange I want one day of your soldiers life too .

SEBASTIAN TO ALUCARD :-

Yeah sure .

•

Alucard by his demonic power bought back Luis alive due to which Louis got Alucard's demonic power . Further Alucard gave power to sebastian army . After two month of battle Golden Wing won from Ralph . All the soldiers of Ralph's army fought bravely but they can't defeat immortal army . Ralph was also died in battle .

CHAPTER FOUR

SEVEN DAYS

WHEN YOU BEGIN A JOURNEY OF REVENGE , START BY DIGGING TWO GRAVES : ONE FOR YOUR ENEMY , AND ONE FOR YOUR YOURSELF .

- JODI PICOULT

ONE WEEK AFTER BATTLE OF SKYRIM ,

Ralph was died in the battle . So , after his death Robert and William took his place as king . Robert and William divide Skyrim into two region Upper and lower . Upper region was ruled by William and lower region was ruled by Robert . After dividing Skyrim into two region it was called "the two thrones Kingdom" . It was first time in history when a kingdom was ruled by two kings . After that they both announced their son as future successor of two thrones . Meanwhile , Sebastian was preparaing for fourth battle of skyrim . Sebastian sent a massenger for declaring war against Skyrim . Robert and William accepted the battle and it will finally be going to happen after three months . Robert and Wlliam set a meeting for battle after one month . They were unaware of Sebastian's demon power yet . They thought that they can easily win the battle . There is a very famous quotes that " A coin has always two face and in this story demonic power is a alternative of angelic power ".

After two months ,

Sebastian left Luis and Olivia in Wister castle under the guidance of Leonard and departured for skyrim . Both Skyrimian angelic army and Wister's demonic army were arrived to battleground . William and Robert both had smile on their faces . They were sure about winning . William sent his army one by one in form of unit but they all were killed and it was surprise for both William and Robert . After an hour William's army was halved and than after half an hour his whole army were killed . William asked for help from Robert . Robert sent his halved army but they were also killed by Wister's demonic army . Robert knew that they had no chance to win so he left the battleground with his remaning army . William tried to escape but it won't worked and he was captured and killed by Sebastian . Now Sebastian is the new king of Skyrim . Sebastian reunited the upper and lower region of Skyrim . William had one son called Tristan . After loosing battle , Tristan was hiding somewhere in Skyrim . Sebastian announced that those who found the Tristan will rewarded one million rio . Sebastian sealed all the docks of Skyrim and made a unit of soldier to find Tristan .

Meanwhile , Leonard made a unit of soldier and appoints Luis as leader of that unit . Leonard sent Luis to Shire for some work purpose . The route of Shire takes one month . Shire is actually a huge island in west side . Shire also called "island of wonders and imagination" due to its historic battle between God Noha and Demon king Alucard . The battle between Noha and Alucard had later built many wonderful monuments and places that a person cannot imagine . It is a beautiful and unique island .

After seven days ,

Sebastian found Tristan hiding in a village . The unit of soldier which was sent behind Tristan were killed by Tristan . After this incident Sebastian himself with his another unit gone on that village . Tristan was ready for Sebastian's attack . Next day , Sebastian arrived to that village . Tristan with no fear on his face came in front of Sebastian . Sebastian sent his soldiers one by one but they all were killed . Sebastian knew that something is suspicious with Tristan . Sebastian figured it out , it must be angelic power . Finally it is time for Sebastian to fight . Fighting was profitable for Sebastian and having a strong chance of winning because of his strong and powerful demonic power . Tristan angelic power was not developed enough to defeat Sebastian demonic power . After a long fight , Tristan was badly injured and exhausted . Than Sebastian give him a strong punch on his face and Tristan fell on ground . Tristan wasn't able to move his body properly . Sebastian was going to kill Tristan with his sword . Tristan lost his hope and thought that it is end of his life than suddenly Sebastian's body stopped responding and he fell in ground . Tristan and everyone else who watching this incident does not understand what's going on . After few minutes Sebastian whole body disappear like dust . After disappearance of Sebastian , every member of Wister's demonic army also disppeared like a dust . Everyone thought that it might be Tristan's strategy . But , Tristan was also clueless about this incident . After the disappearance of Sebastian , Tristan declared himself winner of the fight . After defeating Sebastian in fight , Tristan declared himself the king of skyrim .

Meanwhile in mancay , *Luis was unaware about his father death . After completing his work on mancay , Luis visit some historic places of mancay where he found a temple of Alucard . That temple was sealed by mancay priests . Luis was curious about that temple so he entered that temple by special permission of king of mancay . In temple he found some black magic tool and some rituality symbol on ground . Luis was curious about that temple so he asked natives about that temple they said that ,*

•

NATIVES TO LUIS :-

The association called "black demon" were performing some black magic stuff in that place and the next day they all were found dead . No one knowns their reason of death but there was a rumour that they were devoted to Alucard "the king of demon" and after their prayers , Alucard appear and killed them all . This rumour is actually valid because all the people who found dead on that temple were having black blood .

After one month ,

Luis has arrived to Wister where he found that his father was already died . Luis was broken inside and his body was cradled . It was very emotional moment for Luis because his younger sister Olivia made a drawing of Luis , Olivia and Sebastian together played game in which she marked on Sebastian which resembles the location of sebastian . Next day , Leonard told Luis about Tristan the son of William Hartland and the "new king of Skyrim" .

Next day ,

An unknown source invited Leonard on the subject to negotiate for defeating Tristan in battle . It was very risky invitation because no one knowns about that source from where it came . Luis accepted that invitation and asked Leonard for permission . Leonard agreed for Luis opinion on invitation . Luis and Leonard noticed that something is dubious about invitation . Luis arrived to that place where that unknown source had invited . Luis saw a man coming towards him . He worn a black mask on his head and had a sword on his hand . That man attacked Luis . Luis somehow survived from his attacks . Luis countered every attacks of that man and finally defeated him . That mysterious man fell in ground and begging for mercy . Luis decided to forgive him and asked Leonard for introgation . But , that man take a stone and attack on Luis's face . Luis fell in ground . Than suddenly Leonard arrived and save luis from that mysterious man .

Next day ,

Luis found himself on his room .

Leonard entered Luis's room and asked his condition .

LEONARD TO LUIS :-

What's your condition now ??

LUIS TO LEONARD :-

Better .

Who was that man and what you found .

LEONARD TO LUIS :-

We found nothing about that man and where he came from . But one thing is clear that he wanted us dead . Must be your father's old enemy . Who knowns ?

•

Luis noticed Leonard's injuries and figured it out that Leonard was the one who saved him yesterday . But he had one question on his mind that how he get there so fast within seconds . Next day Luis agian went to that place for investigation where he found black blood on floor and it was not clotted yet . Luis connect this theory of black blood with Mancay's temple incident and thought that the mysterious man was a member of organisation known as black demon .

CHAPTER FIVE

BLACK BLOOD

ALL TRUTHS ARE EASY TO UNDERSTAND ONCE THEY ARE DISCOVERED ; THE POINT IS TO DISCOVER THEM .

- GALILEO GALILEI

Robert was hiding in DANMILTON . Danmilton was another neighbouring country of skyrim . Robert had two son and one daughter . EMILIO was the elder son , LEON was second son of Robert and ELISA was daughter of Robert . Robert used to pay twenty thousand rio for his residential in Danmilton to Danmilton's king ALBERT . Albert was very greedy king . Just like Remy , Albert could do anyhing for his benefites . After two months Robert's royal treasury was emptied and only few to live were left . Albert knew that Robert doesn't have money and he can cheat him as he did earlier with William . Albert decided to kill Robert by the hands of Tristan because Robert betrayed Tristan's father William Hartland . Albert made a plan to arrest Robert and his whole family . Albert sent his son Marcello to arrest Robert and his family . Emilio and Marcello were very close childhood friends . Albert insisted Marcello to arrest his friend's family . Marcello was under the pressure of Albert because Albert threatened Mercello , that if he refuses order than his fiance will die next morning . Marcello was going to do the things against his will . Marcello invited Emilio and his family for dinner . Marcello called assasins to kill Robert's family after dinner . Massenger of Robert on royal family gave him news that "Albert will trying to kill you , stay safe !!" . Robert knew Marcello's plan so he requested Marcello to his house for dinner . Marcello thought if he refuses the invitation then he will be more suspicious to Robert , hence he accepted the invitation . After dinner , Robert's wife served drinks to all soldier who came there to protect Marcello . Robert had mixed poisons in glasses except Marcello's drink because he wanted Marcello as hostage and want to fullfill his demands from Albert . But situation was not going as per the plan because Marcello took Robert's wife . Marcello's soldiers were died due to poison on their drink .

•

MARCELLO TO ROBERT'S FAMILY :-

If anyone of you moves towards me than this lady will no more be alive .

EMILIO TO MARCELLO :-

Leave my mother ,

You are my friend and I know you can never do something like this . We are friends from our childhood . I know your father is forcing you to do so . Think about it , we are friends not an enemy . Drop your weapon and I promise we both will find solution .

MARCELLO TO EMILIO :-

If I won't do this then my father will kill my fiance . I have no other no choice . I have to kill you my friend .

EMILIO TO MARCELLO :-

How can you call me your friend if you want me dead . Do you even know what friend means . Friend is who walks with you whatever the condition will , when world stop accepting you . Friends is not just a word it's our strenght . It is a relationship that can never be seen or touched , it can only be felt .

•

Marcello felt his friendship with Emilio and he became emotional . Marcello threatened Emilio and his family again . But fate wanted something else , Marcello was killed by Leon . But due to Marcello refluxed action Robert's wife was died . Leon thought that if he let Marcello to talk then probably his whole family be died . Emilio unconsciousally and fell in ground . Both mother and friend died in front of Emilio due to his brother Leon . Robert took Emilio away from his home and ordered Leon to run away .

Next day ,

Albert found his son's corprse in Robert's house . Albert ordered his soldier to find Robert and his kids and set two lakh rio bounty those who found them .

Next day ,

Leon and Robert both were separated from each other . Leon was robbed by some robbers . Robbers wanted to kill him but one of them decided to train Leon and make him a part of their group . After two month Leon became a trained and professional assassin .

Meanwhile , Luis arrived to Mancay for investigation of black blood and the incident in Mancay's temple . Mancay's king invited Luis to visit his castle . Luis accepted the invitation . Mancay's show Luis his rest room . After few hour few servant came for the room service . Luis saw one of them mixing poisonous drug into alcohol . Luis saw everything and asked that servant to drink it in front of him . Every servant in that room figured it out that Luis knew about it so they immediately attacked Luis but they all got killed by Luis . Luis was betrayed by Mancay's king . Luis somehow manage to escape from castle and went to prison where he found a prisoner named Richard . Richard requested Luis to help him escape prison and he will give every detail that Luis wanted to . Luis broke the lock of jail and escaped with Richard . After few hour , Luis and Richard both found in Mancay's market . Both were surrounded by Mancay's soldier . Luis saw a prisoner hanging in front of market , that was punishment given by king . That prisoner also requested Luis to set him free from this punishment than he will help him to kill Mancay's soldier . Luis also helped him to escape . Luis , Richard and that prisoner , together they all killed every soldiers present there . Richard help Luis to find name of died member of black demons . Luis shocked when he heard the name of Remy/Raymond on that list .

•

LUIS TO RICHARD :-
Where did you got this list ?
RICHARD TO LUIS :-
It's a long story .

I know you were surprised when you heard name of Raymond/Remy .

LUIS TO RICHARD :-

How you know Remy too .

RICHARD TO LUIS :-

Except Skyrimians no one knowns Raymond as his true name . People called him "white fox" . He was very clever and despicable person I ever saw in my life .

LUIS TO UNKNOWN PRISONER :-

What is your name ?

UNKNOWN PRISONER :-

RUDOLF . My name is Rudolf .

•

Richards made a plan to kidnap Mancay's king and take him as a hostage .

NEXT DAY ,

Richard asked Mancay's king for a buisness deal and development of Mancay . Mancay's king accepted the offer and invited him next day . Richard changed his name to Martin . Richard gave Mancay's king a gift . Mancay's king called one of his servant to send gift in teasury room . From that gift Luis and Rudolf came up and took position in Mancay's king room . After discussion about buisness plan , Mancay's king went to his room . When he arrived to his room suddenly Luis and Rudolf took him as a hostage . Luis interrogated him about the subject of assassination on that temple . Mancay's king finally revealed the truth about assassination . Actually , Leonard was mastermind behind this whole assassination plan . It was a bit suprising for Luis that how can he do that with him . By the help of Mancay's king as hostage Luis and Rudolf easy escaped from mancay .

After one month ,

Luis arrived to Wister . Leonard welcomed Luis and Rudolf . Leonard already knew that if Luis is still alive that means his assassination plan failed and Luis might know about him . After few hour ,

•

LUIS TO LEONARD :-

Why did you want me dead ??

LEONARD TO LUIS :-

You know nothing Luis . What is seen does not happen and what is seen is not seen . They are fool who knows only the truth , but they are smart if they knew difference between truth and falsehood . You heard my name from rumour , you heard my name from incidents . I am thruth behind everything you heard , I am everything that you got , I am behind everything that you built , I am behind everything that you lose . Call me whatever you want but you know me already . I am always there in each and every step . You know me from the beginning but you didn't understood me . I am the one for your cause Because I am you and you are me .

LUIS TO LEONARD :-

Tell me you are not what I am thinking of .

LEONARD TO LUIS :-

MY NAME IS ALUCARD .

I AM THE KING OF DEMONS , AND THAT'S WHAT PEOPLE CALL ME . I AM THE GREATEST ALUCARD THE KING OF DEMONS . DEMON KING ....

Suddenly Richard came ,

RICHARD TO LEONARD/ALUCARD :-

You are behind everything and you are behind everyone . Tell me was Remy a part of your grand plan .

ALUCARD TO RICHARD :-

Yes I am behind everything including Remy too . But Rudolf is not part of my grand plan .

RICHARD TO ALUCARD :-

You bastard !!

•

Richard attacked Alucard but suddenly that place transfered to forest and than desert and than sky and again forest . Richard was cradled on his position . Richard and Luis were shocked by Alucard powers and abilities . Within a persistence of eyes he appeared behind Richard and killed him .

ALUCARD TO LUIS :-

He is no use of me so I killed him .

My power is to convert reality into imagination and imagination into reality . My powers makes me the powerful being ever . I am telling you because You are the most vital source of grand plan . When time come you know everything about my power .

CHAPTER SIX

BETRAYAL

THE DAY NATHAN DIED ,

In this whole story the biggest traitor was Remy .He planned Nathan's death from the very begining . Remi was someone who could do anything for his own benefit . He is such a despicable and rascal person who could sell his own body for other people harm . Ralph thought that Remy was such a rascal who betrayed his most loyal ally for his benefits so why not in future he can do the same with me . Ralph had conversation with one of his loyal assassin to kill Remy . But meanwhile Remy heard all the conversation and ran far away from Skyrim . Remy was hiding in Wister and changed his name from Remy to *Raymond* .

Meanwhile , Ralph set a fifty lakh rio bounty on Remy's head about . Raymond also known as Remy was well settled in Wister as merchant .

After one week ,

Raymond had conversation with thieves and criminals on royal heist in Wister castle . All agreed but only in a condition that they will first free their leader Richard from prison and then proceed the mission .

Next day ,

Raymond with his culpable group attacked the prison . But , Night before attack Raymond planted the bags of sulphur powder on bootcamp of Wister prison guard and when the time came he fired the bags of sulphur powder . Most of them were died due to fire and only few were left and they were killed by thieves and criminal . It was a biggest prison break ever in Wister . News spread all over the Kingdom including Skyrim too . Ralph thought that it could be Remy . Now Raymond revealed his identity to thieves and criminal . After this incident they renamed Remy as *WHITE FOX . Ralph sent his loyal assassin to Wister to find Remy . His assassin noticed that there is something suspicious in Wister . Later on he found that some group of criminals and thieves is made a GROUP to rob royal treasury and their leader is Richard and there is a man called White Fox . Assassin gone for Remy gave this information to Ralph next day . Assassins also joined the team to gather more information .*

The day before royal heist ,

After planning a complete robbery, thay had dinner and all went to sleep on the bed. But few members of team were stayed night , talking about plan after that Richard raised topic about the "demon king" Alucard and told them how powerful he is . Raymond payed full attention on Richard words .Richard said that there is a place in Westerns called Shire where people worship GOD Noha . And also a very famous story about battle of Alucard and Noha , and how god Noha defeated Alucard . Alucard was demon who inherited a very magnificent power . That power was strong enough to take down whole kingdom at once . Alucard is very clever and intelligent king of demon .

Royal Heist day ,

Raymond was merchant in Wister so he proposes an idea of business for king Leonard . King Leonard was very excited for that proposal and invited him for meeting in assembly . Raymond gifted him a box of gold and silver . Leonard accepted that gift and told some of his soldiers to keep that gift inside the treasury . Leonard thought that there is something suspicious about Raymond so he first checked the box but he found nothing dangerous on it . Leonard liked the gift and called some soldiers to put it into treasury . The soldiers were Raymond's ally and got permission to enter the royal treasury . Now then the main plan began . The day before heist , Richard as a worker gone to royal treasury to get map information and planted a bag of sulphur powder in backskirts of treasure room .

Present day ,

Richard fired that bags and a big explosion occurred . Near castle there was a river called Benito . Richard threw gold coin in river as soon as possible . Due to streams of river gold coins were gone far away from castle . After few miles thieves set a net into the river where all the coin got collected .

.

Later on Raymond was arrested by Wister soldier and he surrendered .

•

RAYMOND to LEONARD :-

I am innocent your highness . I am not involved on that heist .

LEONARD to RAYMOND :-

Prove it .

RAYMOND to LEONARD :-

In this whole scenerio I was always with you and not even ran away .

Heist is just a coincience . I can help you to find the hideout of that criminals .

LEONARD(with order) to RAYMOND :-

I will give seven days for investigation .

RAYMOND(with respect) :-

Yes your highness .

After seven day ,

RAYMOND to LEONARD :-

I found them . They are seven mile ahead from here hiding on a dungeon .

Follow the river Benito and then took right turn about three mile than you will found a dungeon and there they are .

CHAPTER SEVEN

END OF PROLOGUE

DAY OF POSSESSION ,

When the soldiers investigated that temple they all found that victims blood was pure black . They also found the body of Remy/Raymond and declared that all victims are dead . When Ralph himself visited that place and recognised Remy's body and declared that Remy is dead . Leonard was also shocked by the news of Raymond's death because he was loyal to him .

ONE MONTH AFTER RAYMOND'S DEATH ,

After dinner , Leonard was going to bed and saw Raymond's body on his bed . He got scared and locked his room from outside . He slept outside the room till the midnight until he saw a dream of Raymond hunting him and trying to kill him . But he thought that it was just a dream so he entered the room , than suddenly Remy appeared Leonard thought that it might be his dream but when Raymond started to convert into demon king Alucard ! then he realised that all this scenario is happening in reality . Now Raymond completely converted into Alucard . Leonard scared and ran away from his room than suddenly he saw that Raymond standing in front of him . Then he ran away in opposite side to Alucard but , Alucard teleported there instantly . Leonard was begging for his life but Alucard refused and ruthlessly stabbed him and in result Leonard died . Then he touched Leonard corpse and within a second he converted himself into Leonard . Then he buried Leonard corpse far from castle . But meanwhile , a servent named John saw the incident and next day he left that castle and said he will never return .

PRESENT DAY ,

ALUCARD TO LUIS :-

Always remember our plan " DEUS MORTEM NOHA (DEATH OF NOHA) " .

NEXT DAY ,

Somewhere in Danmilton's *forest ,*

Tribes of Danmilton found Luis in forest and rescued him . Meanwhile , after knowing that Luis and Leonard both were missing from Wister . Albert planned to attack Wister and add Wister in Danmilton kingdom . Robert along with his son Leon were missing from Danmilton . Emilio was hiding in HISEN . Hisen was a kingdom famous for gladiator fights .

<u>NOTE :-</u>

<u>1.TIMEO AUTEM MEDITATI (T.A.M)</u>

" TIMEO AUTEM MEDITATI " IS A POWER TO CONVERT IMAGINATION INTO REALITY AND REALITY INTO IMAGINATION . ALUCARD INHERITED POWER OF TAM . THERE IS CERTAIN BOUNDRIES

BETWEEN IMAGINATION AND REALITY CALLED "TERMINUS ILLUD ". USER OF TAM PUT VICTIM BETWEEN IMAGINATION AND REALITY . USER MAKES VICTIM TO IMAGINE THE SCENE ON USER WILL AND IN THIS CONDITION VICTIM WILL DO SAME AS USER WANT IN REALITY . AND WHEN VICTIM LOOSES HIS WILL USER GET A CHANCE TO EASILY KILL VICTIM . TAM IS A INHERITED POWER WHICH PASSED ON GENRATION TO GENERATION .

•

2. DEMON BRIMIR

BRIMIR IS A IMAGINATED SWORD OF ALUCARD THAT BECAME REAL ON FIGHT BETWEEN GOD NOHA AND DEMON KING ALUCARD .

•

TO BE CONTINUED....

•

----YOU HAVE COMPLETED FIRST PART OF THIS STORY----

-- SANSKAR AND SANKALP VAISHNAV

-------------------------THANK YOU-----------------------

9 798886 064582

Printed by Libri Plureos GmbH in Hamburg,
Germany